When LiYAH Gets Carried Away

Loraine Joseph

Illustrated by
Laura Fernandez

ISBN 978-1-953194-83-1

Published by Believe In Your Book Publishing

Printed in the United States of America

For permission request, write to the publisher, addressed
"Attention: Permissions Coordinator/ to the address below.

Email: Info@BelieveInYourBook.com

To my loving husband Ismail
and my dear children Jeremiah, Jaliyah, and Janiyah
Thank you for the push, the drive, and the inspiration.

Liyah sits at her desk, staring at the clock, waiting for school to end.

It is a sunny Friday afternoon in Ms. Flowers' second-grade class. Liyah is very excited about the weekend. All she could think about is how much fun it would be to play on the playground, slide down the slide, swing on the swings, and eat chocolate ice cream.

She is pulled from her daydream.

"Finally!" Liyah whispers to herself as she stuffs her notebook and pencils in her backpack.

"Class!" Ms. Flowers calls out. "Remember to practice your power words for our spelling test on Monday! If you want to get an A, you must-"

"- study, study, study!" the students say altogether.

As Liyah walks toward the front of the school, she spots her dad from a distance. She runs toward him in excitement.

"Daddy!"
she calls out.

"Hey, Liyah how was school today?"

"School was okay," she replies with a shrug.

"Just okay?" asks dad.

"Yeah, we have a spelling test on Monday and Ms. Flowers said that we must study, study, study if we want to get an A!"

Dad laughs at Liyah's expression, "Ms. Flowers is right, you know.
Sometimes you play too much and get carried away.
Be sure you take time to practice your words and **not** procrastinate."

"Huh, pro-cras-ti-nate?" Liyah says slowly.
"Hmmm, that's a big word daddy!"

"Yes, it is. It means to keep putting off something that should be done. Do you think you can spell it?" Liyah thinks for a minute.

"Uhh...
p-r-o
-c-r-a-s-t
-i-n-a
-t-e?"

"You got it Liyah! I knew you could do it!" her dad says.

"So does this mean I can get ice cream?" she asks.

"Maybe another time sweetheart," her dad chuckles. "I have some work to finish up when we get home."

As dad opens the door Liyah rushes through and throws her backpack on the floor. She thinks to herself how she can't wait to start her weekend. Before she could race upstairs to her bedroom, her mom calls out from the kitchen.

"Whoa, Liyah, slow down. How was school today?" she asks.

"Hi, mommy! School was great. I have to study for a spelling test on Monday. Daddy explained to me that I should not procrastinate.
p-r-o
-c-r-a-s-t
-i-n-a
-t-e
procrastinate."

Her mom snickers and nods.
"Ah, I see. Since you know what it means, use your time wisely.
And remember your brother is doing his homework so you have to be-"

"-Shhh, quiet!"
She says with a smile as she is anxious to get to her toys.

She looks around her room and notices all her toys and stuffed animals lying around, just the way she left them before school.
Liyah throws her backpack down and quickly walks toward her dolls and begins to play.

"I'll just play for a little while," she tells herself.

"How is it going Liyah?" her dad asks as he peeps his head through the door.

"Uhh...I know, I know, I won't procrastinate." Liyah takes out her notebook, she attempts to do her words, but she doesn't.

"Liyah, it's dinner time!" her mom calls out from downstairs.

"How's the studying coming along Liyah?" her mom asks.

"I'll study as soon as I get back upstairs. I got a little carried away playing."

But before Liyah knows it, the night drags on, and she grows tired. Soon it's too late to study for her spelling test.

"Yawn, I'll study first thing in the morning."
Then off to bed she goes.

On Saturday morning, during breakfast, dad reminds Liyah to not wait until the last minute to get her work done.

"I'll get to it!" she says.

Mom looks at Liyah and adds, "Remember, it's easy to get carried away especially when you have other things to do."

"Yup, that's true. I'll get to it," Liyah says again with a silly grin.

So after breakfast, Liyah sits in her bedroom and begins to study her words. Her brother, Jeremiah helps. A few minutes later Liyah hears her friend Zoey calling out from her bedroom window.

"Liyah! Liyah! Come outside and play."

"Sorry Zoey, not today, I have a spelling test on Monday!" Liyah says.

"Come on, Liyah. Just for a little while?" Zoey pleads.
"Come see my new bike, we could have a race! See if you can keep up at my pace."

Liyah gets excited and needs no more encouragement. With helmet and knee pads in place, she zooms downstairs for a fun race.

"Not again, I got carried away!"

"Did you clean your room?" mom calls out from downstairs.

"I'm doing it now!" Liyah tells her mom.

"I have to clean up this mess then study for my test," she tells herself lazily.

The next morning, Liyah jumps out of bed. "It's Sunday already! At last, time to study!"

But, a few minutes later, her dad cries out, "Liyah! It's time to go. We have errands to run!"

"The day has passed and the sun has set. I didn't get time to study yet," Liyah whispers sadly to herself.

"Good morning, boys and girls!" Ms. Flowers says cheerfully. "I hope you all had a great weekend. Let's get ready for our test."

"If only I used my time wisely," Liyah scolds herself.

After school, Ms. Flowers calls Liyah over to her desk.
    "Liyah, what happened?"

Tears stream down Liyah's cheek.
    "I didn't study," she explains regretfully.
    "I spent my entire weekend procrastinating."

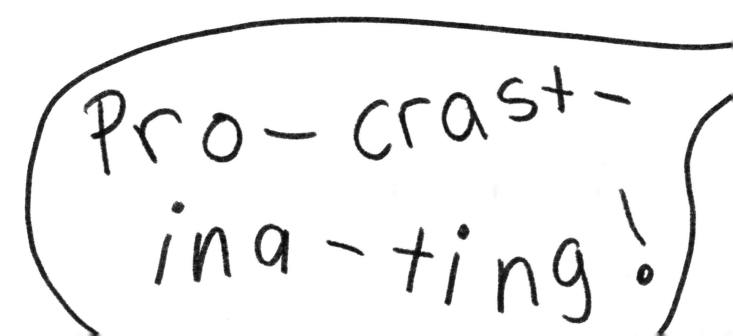

"Wow! That's a fancy word Liyah." Ms. Flowers says.

"My dad taught me," Liyah replies as she wipes her cheeks every few seconds.

"Well it's true. I hope next time you won't procrastinate," encourages Ms. Flowers.

"You must learn when it is the right time to play and when it's the right time to get your work done. Procrastination stops you from doing the things you need to do."

"I'm going to give you a second chance," Ms. Flowers graciously says.

"Thank you," Liyah replies, "I promise not to get carried away next time."

Later that week, Liyah did just that. When she was given something to do, she did not wait until the last minute. She got right to it.

"Like my daddy always says….

...if you have something to do,
don't get carried away,
so when you're through,
you'll have more time to play!"

About the Author

As a native of sunny South Florida, Loraine Joseph is an educator, a writer, and mentor. Growing up, she had a creative imagination and a love for writing. That passion inspired her to create books that foster morality, develop empathy, encourage imagination, and spark natural curiosity. When she's not writing or teaching, she enjoys traveling, crafting, and spending time with those she loves. She lives in Florida with her loving husband and three beautiful children.